The rain had stopped, replaced by a heavy mist. There, in the mist, lit by a single lantern, was a black, horse-drawn cart. It looked like one of those old-fashioned hearses Jeff had seen carrying coffins in movies. Jeff's heart began to pound right through his chest. The hearse was heading his way.

But what Jeff saw next almost made him scream—there was a man dressed in a black suit driving the cart. Jeff couldn't see his face at first. Then the man leaned forward and Jeff gasped. His face was the most hideous sight he had ever seen. It was almost as if the man were a living skeleton.

Jeff was too terrified to move. Then he heard the man speak and saw him stretch out his arm.

"Come," the man said in a slow, haunting voice. "It's time."

The
Scariest Stories
You've Ever Heard,
PART III

The Scariest Stories
You've Ever Heard,
PART III

by Tracey E. Dils

cover illustration by Richard Kriegler

To my baby sister, Rebecca,
who still can't sleep with the lights off
because of all the scary stories I told her

⋐PAGES⋑

Sixth printing by Willowisp Press 1996.

Published by Willowisp Press
801 94th Avenue North, St. Petersburg, Florida 33702

Printed in the United States of America

6 8 10 9 7

ISBN 0-87406-515-1

Contents

INTRODUCTION

You're the only one home. A storm has been raging outside your window all evening. The lights in your house flicker off, then on, then off again—for good. You fumble in the drawer for a flashlight, but you can't find one. You feel around in the cupboard for a candle, but there are none there. You pick up the phone. The line is dead.

The lightning outside flashes an eerie glow throughout the room. In the split second of the lightning flash, you see someone—or something—at the top of your stairs heading down. You're paralyzed for a minute. The thing moves closer. It's now at the bottom of the stairs. You turn and run for the front door. You turn the knob, but somehow, the front door is jammed. You think about heading to the back door—but the thing is between you and the back door. It's getting closer, closer. You reach for the knob one more time, praying that the door will open. The thing is almost to you now, its arms outstretched. You turn the knob. Miraculously, the door opens. You run outside, slamming the door behind you. You've barely escaped from something so unspeakable that you can hardly imagine what it would have been like if it had caught you!

You probably know how this feels. Everyone has been terrified by something at some time. Usually, whatever you are afraid of isn't real—it's a product of your imagination. You may have seen a scary movie that started you thinking about scary things. Or you may have read a frightening book that made you jumpy. But usually you get scared because you've let your imagination run wild. And there's really nothing wrong with that. After all, your imagination can do wonderful things—and every once in a while, it scares you. That's part of its job.

The stories in this book are the products of my imagination. None of them actually happened. Most of them could never really happen. But scary stories work best if they sound as if they are true. If you are sharing these with your friends, or telling them around a campfire or at your next slumber party, you may want to change them a bit so that they sound as if they happened to you.

The couple in "Killer Cactus" could be your older sister and her husband. The incident at the camp in the story "Horror Weekend" could have happened at your very own summer camp. And "Dead Man's Hill" could even be a hill in your town. Don't be afraid to change some of the details to make the stories even scarier. Don't be afraid to let your imagination take these stories in totally different directions.

Many of the stories in this book are about things that have scared me at different times in my life. And, as I wrote these stories, I discovered something wonderful about scary things. Writing stories about them made them less scary! You might want to try to write some scary stories yourself. Pick something that you're really scared of and then write a story about it and see what happens. You might even want to read the story out loud to your friends to see if you can scare them. You may even want to put together a whole book of your own scary stories.

Just remember, being scared isn't so bad. In fact, it's kind of fun. So dim the lights in your room. Pull your covers up under your chin. And open this book—if you dare. And remember to tell yourself—it's only a story, it's only a story.

Hide-and-Seek

ERIC Jones loved the house that he and his mother had moved into. It was a far cry from the cramped apartment that they had lived in in New York City. Their new house was in a little village in Vermont. When Eric looked out of his window, he didn't see the dirty streets of Manhattan below him—instead he saw green, rolling hills.

And the house was huge, too. It had been built at the turn of the century and had three fireplaces and wonderful high ceilings. There was a great front parlor with a winding staircase and five large bedrooms. But the best part of all was the stables—there would be a place to put a horse, if he could talk his mother into letting him have one!

The only thing that bothered Eric was what he had heard about the house from Old

Man Mackinbecker, his new next-door neighbor. On the day they had moved in, Eric and his mother had gone next door to introduce themselves. Mr. Mackinbecker had seemed nice enough. But when he heard that they had bought the house next door, his face had turned white. He'd bought that house himself, he explained, years ago, as a wedding gift to his bride. They were to have gotten married in the front parlor. But on the day of the wedding, she disappeared and had never been heard from again.

Eric and his mom listened carefully as Mr. Mackinbecker told the story. The bride had been trying to hide from her new husband because she didn't want him to see her before the wedding. Before he knew it, everyone was playing a game of hide-and-seek—even the bridesmaids! But when Mr. Mackinbecker's bride hid, no one could find her. Sixty years had passed and no one had ever seen her again.

Mr. Mackinbecker figured that she had never wanted to marry him in the first place and had run away to get out of the whole mess. But whatever had happened, Eric could tell that it had left Mr. Mackinbecker heartbroken. Mr. Mackinbecker explained that he knew he could never live in the house and sold it immediately. He had moved next door. But the new owners had never moved in. And no one had lived there until Eric and his mother had moved in that day.

It was a weird story, all right, a weird story that Eric tried not to think about, especially at night. But what was even weirder were the sounds that he had started hearing at night before he went to bed. They were hard to describe. They sounded a little like scratching. Then they would grow louder, turning into pounding noises. And they came from directly above his room, from somewhere in the attic. The first time he had heard them, he had gotten his mother and asked her to come into his room. But the sounds had stopped by the time she had gotten there. She had insisted that it had been his imagination. He'd heard it again the next night and called to his mom, but again the sounds had stopped as soon as she walked into the room.

One night, when Eric's mother was out for the evening and Eric was home alone, the sounds grew louder than ever. The pounding got more and more intense until the ceiling of Eric's room began to shake. Eric was really frightened—but he couldn't think of anything to do! If he called his mom, he would ruin her date. And she probably wouldn't believe him anyway.

I know, Eric thought to himself. *I'll go over to Mr. Mackinbecker's. He'll know what to do.* He grabbed his bathrobe, put on his tennis shoes, and headed next door.

After he knocked on Mr. Mackinbecker's front door, he realized how stupid he was being. If his own mom didn't believe him, why would Mr. Mackinbecker? He decided to go back home. But by then it was too late. Mr. Mackinbecker answered the door.

"I'm sorry to bother you so late," Eric began. Then he decided that since he was already there, he might as well tell the whole story. When Eric was all finished, Mr. Mackinbecker shook his head.

"Well, son, I don't rightly know what you've been hearing. But if it were me, I sure would be investigating what was up there. Probably rats or bats or squirrels, but I'd sure want to know. They can all do some damage to an attic."

Eric thought for a second. There was no way that he would go into that attic by himself. He looked at Mr. Mackinbecker with pleading eyes.

"Do you want me to go with you?" Mr. Mackinbecker asked.

Eric nodded.

"You know I haven't set foot in that house for 60 years, don't you?"

Eric nodded again. "Mr. Mackinbecker, please, you have to go with me. My mom doesn't believe me and I just have to find out what's making those noises."

"Okay, okay," Mr. Mackinbecker said. "I guess I'm probably old enough to pretend that I don't remember what happened there. Just let me get my coat and a flashlight."

When Mr. Mackinbecker returned, the two of them crossed the yard to Eric's house.

They stopped in Eric's room first and, sure enough, there was the sound. Only this time, it was a light pounding only every once in a while. It was almost like whoever was making the noise had become tired.

"Well, my boy," Mr. Mackinbecker said. "You know what we've got to do."

They headed to the door that led to the attic.

They began walking up the attic stairs. They hadn't heard the pounding for several minutes now, but Eric was still shaking.

Whoever—or whatever—was making that sound was somewhere up there, waiting.

They reached the top and looked around. There were a few old pieces of furniture covered with dust and some old boxes. Mr. Mackinbecker turned his flashlight on what looked like a figure in the corner. Eric gasped. It was a person! A person all dressed in white.

Mr. Mackinbecker chuckled. "Just an old dressmaker's dummy, nothing to be afraid of. Now, let's see, your room is right underneath that corner over there, see, right by that old trunk. Come on! Let's see if we can't scare us up some rats!"

Eric followed Mr. Mackinbecker to the corner of the attic where the trunk was. Neither of them heard a sound—no pounding, no scratching, nothing.

"Here's your answer," Mr. Mackinbecker said. "There's probably a nest of rats in this here trunk! Let's open it up and see."

Eric's palms became clammy. He sure didn't want to see a trunk full of rats, that's for sure, but it was better than imagining what terrible thing was making that noise.

Mr. Mackinbecker jiggled the lock on the trunk. "Hmmm. The lock's pretty tight and this trunk seems real solid. But rats have been known to eat through anything!"

Mr. Mackinbecker pulled at the lock again, but it wouldn't budge. Eric pulled a Swiss army knife out of his pocket.

"Here, will this help?" he asked.

Mr. Mackinbecker took the knife and worked on the lock. Suddenly, it sprung open.

"Are you ready, my boy? Rats aren't very pretty you know."

Mr. Mackinbecker opened the lid of the trunk. Eric closed his eyes for just a second. When he opened them, he expected to see hundreds of squirming rats.

But what he saw was far, far worse. He heard Old Man Mackinbecker scream.

In the trunk, dressed in a beautiful, ivory satin wedding dress, with a lace veil covering a shock of gray hair, was a skeleton. Its arms were outstretched as if it had been pounding the inside of the trunk. And on the inside of the trunk lid, there were long, bloody scratch marks.

The look on Mr. Mackinbecker's face told Eric all that he needed to know. It was the skeleton of Mr. Mackinbecker's bride. They had found her hiding place. And she had been trying to get out of the trunk for 60 years.

Dead Man's Hill

DEAD Man's Hill had been a legend around Willsburg for as long as anyone could remember. It was a medium-sized sloping hill on the edge of town. There weren't any houses on Dead Man's Hill. Mostly it was a place for town picnics or long walks. Some of the younger boys in town would take their dirt bikes and four-wheelers up the hill and ride through the paths that crisscrossed its crest—but only during the day. Hardly anyone visited Dead Man's Hill at night.

The legend of Dead Man's Hill was just too frightening. Most people figured that the legend probably wasn't true. But what if it was? Most of the kids around Willsburg knew that it was best not to take any chances.

Someone had died on Dead Man's Hill almost 50 years ago. The whole thing had started out as a club initiation—just a few boys daring each other to ride their motorcycles to the edge of the hill and then to make the sharp turn just before they reached the edge of the cliff. The rocky crags on the hill's other side were treacherous. Any rider who didn't make the turn in time would fall to a terrible death. And that's just what happened that night.

According to the legend, young Greg Thompson had not wanted to join his buddies, Tom and Larry, on their nightly ride around the hill. But they had taunted him and called him a chicken. Since he was the newest member of their club, he had wanted to prove himself. There was nothing worse than being called a chicken. So he had taken their dare to rev his motorcycle and head down the hill toward the curve at breakneck speed. He was supposed to turn his motorcycle just in time—but he hadn't. He had kept going. His unearthly scream broke the night as he plunged over the cliff. And when Tom and Larry found him, his neck was broken and his head was twisted completely around.

But that wasn't the worst part of the legend. The worst part was to happen four days later, the night of Greg's funeral. That night, Tom and Larry had been found dead in their beds, their heads twisted completely around.

There were no signs of forced entry, no signs of struggle, no signs of any weapons at either of their homes—just the boys themselves, their bodies horribly contorted. Whoever—or whatever—had done this to the boys had been stronger than any man.

People said that Greg Thompson's ghost had come back from the dead to seek revenge on the boys who had taunted him. And some people said that Greg's ghost still haunted Dead Man's Hill and the treacherous curve. But nobody really knew if the legend was true or not.

It was this legend that Jason Bowman told Andy Johnston one lonely summer night in Willsburg. Andy was new in town and didn't know how seriously to take his new friend. Jason said that it was up to every new kid in town to take a spin on Dead Man's Hill just to prove he was man enough for the town of Willsburg.

Andy had come to town with a new dirt bike—and Jason had just gotten a new ATV. The sun wouldn't set for some time now. It seemed like a perfect night for trail riding and for Andy to prove that he was no chicken. Jason's eyes lit up as he told Andy about the awesome, rocky paths. Before Andy knew it, they were heading for Dead Man's Hill, as the sun was dipping lower and lower in the horizon.

Andy tried to put the legend out of his mind as his dirt bike approached the crest of the hill. He knew that the famous downhill run, with the sharp curve and craggy bluffs, lay on the other side. Jason was behind him and shouted over the noise of their motorcycles, "Time to prove you're a man!"

Andy shook his head. Just then, he caught a glimpse of a figure lurking in the trees—a dark figure, heading his way.

"Hey, who's that guy?" Jason asked. "Maybe he's up for the Dead Man's Hill challenge, too."

"I don't know," Andy answered as the figure came closer. "I'm new here, remember?"

Andy could see now that the figure was a boy about his age dressed in some old clothes that looked like they came from the Salvation Army. Andy couldn't see the guy very well in the dark, but it looked as if his eyes were bloodshot. And his skin seemed to glow faintly in the fading twilight.

"Can either of you guys give me a ride into town?" the figure asked, gesturing to the dirt bike and the ATV. "Some of my friends dropped me off up here—it was sort of a joke, you know?"

"Sure," Jason said with a glint in his eye. "But first, we're going to try this old curve at 60 miles per hour, right, Andy?" Andy just looked down at the ground.

"You're not a real man unless you can take the curve of Dead Man's Hill, you know," Jason said. "At least you should give it a try." Andy nodded his head weakly.

The stranger smiled. "Hey, I know all about Dead Man's Hill. You know what's even better than taking the curve solo, don't you?" he asked.

Jason shook his head.

"Taking that run two at a time! The extra weight really makes you fly down that hill. If you can make the curve with two on board, then you know you're really tough."

Andy looked at his dirt bike and then at Jason's four-wheeler. He knew how dangerous it was to ride two on a four-wheeler. After all, it wasn't that safe to ride on one by yourself. But he could tell by the look in Jason's eyes that this stunt was just one more in the list of stunts that Jason felt would make him cool, make him a man. Andy couldn't believe that this strange kid would want to join them on this insane stunt.

"Well," Jason said to the stranger, hesitating only a little. "Climb aboard."

"Jason . . . ," Andy started. "Maybe you'd better not . . ."

"Geez," Jason said. "Once a wimp, always a wimp. Come on," he gestured to the stranger. "Hop on."

The stranger climbed onto the ATV behind Jason. Andy looked down at his hands on the handlebars of his dirt bike. They were shaking slightly.

"You want to race, or what?" Jason asked Andy.

"Nah," Andy said. "I think I'll just watch you guys try it first. You know, see how it's done."

"Okay, wimp!" Jason said, taking off with the red-eyed stranger behind him.

Andy watched as Jason revved his four-wheeler. The ATV began heading down the slope. It was then that Andy saw the most hideous sight he had ever seen.

The stranger was transforming himself right in front of Andy's eyes. First, the stranger's eyes popped out of his head, and then bloody blue and red veins popped from his face. The skin seemed to peel away by itself, almost like an orange, revealing pink muscles beneath. And then the muscles began peeling away, dripping blood.

Andy took off on his bike behind Jason—he

26

had to warn him before it was too late. He had to make him get off his four-wheeler before he got to the curve!

But it was too late. By the time they reached the end of the slope, the stranger was no more than a skeleton, a laughing, hideous skeleton, with his bony hands around Jason's neck. The skeleton was twisting poor Jason's neck around and around. As the two headed for the cliff, Andy knew that they couldn't turn off in time. He held his breath and closed his eyes. The next sound he heard was a scream—and an unearthly laugh. And then Andy heard words he would never forget. "You're next!" a voice whispered. "You're next!"

When they found Jason the next day, his head was completely turned around, facing backward. Andy tried to tell everyone that the legend of Dead Man's Hill would come full circle, that the skeleton would claim another victim. He even tried to get his parents to move out of town or to send him to live with his grandmother in another town. Anything to escape the horrible fate of those whispered words—*You're next! You're next!*

But no one believed Andy. They all thought he was just shaken up by Jason's death. His parents told him that his imagination was running wild, that he had had a bad scare and needed to take it easy for a while.

No one believed Andy's story of the horrible stranger who lured Jason to his death. At least not until the morning after Jason's funeral. That was when they found Andy's body in his bed, his neck broken, his head completely turned around. On his face was a look of unspeakable horror.

The Secret of the Dollhouse

IT was a very special dollhouse. Melissa knew that the minute her grandmother had shown it to her. It was an exact replica of her grandmother's house, where Melissa lived with her parents, grandparents, and little brother. The house was plenty big enough for all of them. The dollhouse was exactly like the real house, right down to the fancy shutters and wood trim on the outside. And all the rooms matched the rooms in her grandmother's house. Every detail was exactly right, from the rose wallpaper in the front hall to the tiny chandelier in the dining room to the miniature violin in the parlor.

Melissa loved to play with the dollhouse. There was a whole family of dolls—a mother and a father doll, a tiny baby doll, a sister doll, and a grandmother and grandfather doll. Her grandmother would sit in the big kitchen knitting while Melissa played with the doll-house. Her grandmother's knitting needles clinked softly against each other, while oat-meal cookies baked in the oven.

Melissa especially liked that the sister doll seemed to look just like her. It had curly brown hair, brown eyes, and freckles.

Melissa would create her own world in that dollhouse. She imagined what it would be like to be that tiny—to be able to make an entire meal out of a pea, to have picnics with grapes as watermelons, to use tiny bits of thread to knit into sweaters.

As Melissa got older, she played with the dollhouse less often than she did as a young child. Her grandmother would still sit in the kitchen and knit as the cookies baked in the oven. But Melissa had other things to do. She had trees to climb, phone calls to make, parties to plan, and, later, boys to meet. The dollhouse sat in the corner of the kitchen, for-gotten, until her grandmother finally carried the house to the attic. But her grandmother still sat in the same rocker, knitting and bak-ing, and glancing every once in a while at the empty space on the table where the dollhouse had stood.

One day when Melissa was away working as a camp counselor for the summer, she received an urgent call from her mother. Her grandmother had died suddenly of a heart attack. Melissa was heartbroken. She went home for the funeral, but couldn't stay in her grandmother's house. It just wasn't the same without her grandmother there, sitting in the kitchen in her rocker with the cookies baking. It was only years later, after she was finished with college, that she could bring herself to think about her grandmother without bursting into tears.

But, after she had her own daughter, Melissa began to think about those special days in her grandmother's kitchen, with the warm smell of oatmeal cookies filling the air. She wanted to take her own daughter to that house, to show her the special spot where she had played long ago with the dolls in the miniature house in the kitchen.

Her parents had moved to Florida, so Melissa had to think of a special excuse to drive the 180 miles to her grandmother's hometown. She said something about an auction to her husband and drove through the countryside to her grandmother's town, her blond-haired, blue-eyed, seven-year-old daughter Emily in the seat beside her. As she rode, she told Emily stories about the giant house—and about the tiny house that was a perfect copy.

"How big was the dollhouse, Mommy?" Emily asked.

"Well, it wasn't too big. But it was just exactly like my granny's house."

"Did it have a mommy doll?" she asked.

"Yes, and a sister doll and a baby doll and a daddy doll and a grandmother and grandfather doll," Melissa added, her eyes filling with tears. "And the sister doll looked just like me."

When they caught sight of the hill where her grandmother lived, Melissa gasped. The house was in ruins. A section of the roof had fallen in and the foundation was crumbling. She knew that her parents had sold the house after her grandmother had died. But she had no idea that the present owners would let it fall into such disrepair. She pulled the car into the driveway and ran from the car to the house. Emily followed, confused at her mother's reaction.

"Is this it?" Emily asked, disappointed.

Melissa just looked at her daughter and shook her head.

"This is it," she said. "But I don't know what happened."

"Oh, well," Emily said with a grin on her face. "Let's check it out."

As they reached the door, Melissa said to

her daughter, "Surely no one could live here now, the way this place looks." She turned the doorknob. The door was unlocked. "Let's take a look inside."

Together, the two of them explored the house. They wandered around the first floor where the rose wallpaper was peeling off the walls and the chandelier was hanging from the ceiling by a single link of chain. And then they tried the second floor, though Melissa made Emily stay below until she was sure it was safe.

The second floor was as bad as the first—wallpaper was peeling and dust covered everything. When they came to the door that led to the attic, Melissa figured they should turn back—it was all too painful for her. But Emily urged her on. "Come on, Mom, let's look for the dollhouse. Didn't you say that your grandmother put it in the attic?"

Melissa and Emily climbed the stairs and surveyed the big attic room. The roof had caved in in places and the sun shone through the openings.

Melissa gasped when she saw it. There, in the corner of the attic, bathed in a beam of sunlight, was the dollhouse. Somehow it had escaped the collapsing roof. The fancy shutters and wood trim were all in perfect condition.

Emily rushed to the corner where the dollhouse stood.

"Wow, Mom!" she said. "It's just as neat as you said it was! Let's take it home with us!"

Melissa followed her daughter, still not believing that the dollhouse had actually stayed in one piece while the rest of the house had turned to rubble.

Melissa's eyes darted from tiny room to tiny room. There was the violin lying on the mantel of the parlor, just as she had left it the last time she had played with the dollhouse. There was the rose wallpaper, as bright pink as she remembered. There was the chandelier, shining brightly and proudly from the ceiling of the dining room. The table was set, as if the doll family that lived in the house were expecting company.

It was then that she noticed the smell. Floating through the air in the attic was that smell she knew so well—the smell of oatmeal cookies baking in the oven. And when Melissa looked in the kitchen, she saw that the rocking chair, her grandmother's rocking chair, was actually moving slightly, as if the doll had been rocking in it. *Emily must have bumped it,* she thought.

But then Melissa heard, very faintly, the sound of knitting needles. There was no doubt about the sound—she would know it anywhere.

"Hey, Mom," Emily said, breaking into her thoughts. "I thought you said the sister doll looked just like you, with brown hair and brown eyes and freckles."

"That's right," Melissa answered. "There was only one sister and she looked just like me."

"Well, here's the sister doll," said Emily, holding the doll out to Melissa. "And she doesn't look like you at all."

Melissa took the little doll from Emily. The doll had long blond hair and bright blue eyes.

"The sister doll looks just like me," whispered Emily.

The Slasher

HE was staring at her again. Even when she looked down at her newspaper, Sarah could feel his eyes looking vacantly at her, boring a hole through her head.

It had been going on now for 15 minutes, ever since she had gotten on the subway downtown. The two men were already in the car when she boarded. One man in a blue suit sat facing her, staring straight at her, his hands stiffly folded on his lap, his legs stretched in front of him, unmoving.

The other man seemed to be sleeping. He was slouched on the seat of the subway with his eyes closed. His hand was dangling carelessly behind the other man's back. But Sarah could tell he wasn't really asleep. It was more like he was in a daze. He would open one eye every once in a while and look at his friend in the blue suit, as if checking on him to see if he was all right. *They're probably drunk or on drugs,* thought Sarah.

Sarah hadn't really wanted to take the subway. But she'd missed the last bus because she had studied too late. The subway wasn't a very friendly place in the daytime. But at night? Forget it! The subway station was dark and dirty. And the train itself was lit by an eerie green light that made everything and everybody look pale—almost like they were dead.

And the sounds—they were the worst part. First there was the steady clackety clack as the subway train bumped down the dark tunnel—and then a loud screech as it pulled into a station. Finally, there was a low and painful groan, as if a body had just given up its soul.

But Sarah especially didn't want to take the subway because of the story that was going around. The newspapers were full of the subway slasher, a ruthless murderer who lurked in subway cars at night. The slasher picked empty cars and waited inside for people to board. Then he took a seat behind them and put a knife through their backs!

It's just a story, Sarah thought to herself as the train clacked over the tracks through the dark. After all, no one had really seen the slasher. So there'd been a couple of murders—

so what? In a city the size of this one, there were murders every day.

Just four more stops, Sarah told herself. *If I can just get through three more stops, I'll be home.* But another voice seemed to be saying to her, *The man in the blue suit is still staring, he's still staring! Make him stop!*

She glanced at her newspaper again. She looked up. The staring man's weird eyes hadn't moved. They were still gazing right at her. The other man still seemed sort of dazed and out of it. She looked at her newspaper one more time. She looked up. He was still looking at her with a leer in his eyes. She looked around the car. She was alone with the two men. If the guy that was staring at her tried something, if he really was the slasher, she'd be helpless!

The rumbling of the subway began to slow just a bit. That meant they were coming into a station. Sarah braced herself for the horrible screech. It came, followed by the low, unearthly groan. Sarah looked out of the window at the station platform. *Maybe they'll get off here,* she said to herself. *Maybe I should get off here.* But Sarah knew this wasn't a good part of town. Maybe she would be safer here in the subway with these two weirdos than she would be in the subway station. After all, they weren't doing anything. They were just weird. The city was full of weird people.

The men stayed on the train. The car groaned and began to roll again. The man in the blue suit still stared straight at her, his eyes unblinking. His skin seemed to have grown paler still, almost greenish in the subway's odd light.

The other man moaned, checked his friend, and closed his eyes again.

The train screeched and then groaned to a stop again. Sarah held her breath. The doors opened. A nice-looking older gentleman with a briefcase entered the car. He nodded to Sarah and sat down next to her. Now the man in the blue suit was staring at both of them.

The old man fiddled with his briefcase. He looked up. The man in the blue suit stared straight ahead. The old man reached inside his coat and pulled out a pen. The man in the blue suit stared straight ahead. The man next to Sarah took out a pad of paper from his briefcase. The man still stared straight ahead. The older man scribbled something on the pad and pushed it across his briefcase to Sarah.

Sarah looked at the note. It read,

You must get off at the next stop.
Ask no questions. Just follow me.

Sarah looked at the old man with a questioning look in her eyes. He just nodded his head.

The man in the blue suit stared straight ahead. His expression seemed more leering and frightening than ever.

Sarah thought for a second. She had two choices. She could stay on the subway with the two strange men or she could get off at the next stop with a total stranger who seemed— well, nice enough. But she didn't know him. What if *he* was the slasher that she'd read about in the papers? Maybe this is how he lured his victims.

Sarah looked at the old man. Then she looked at the man in the blue suit, with his hollow, staring eyes and strange expression. She realized that she had no choice at all. When the car groaned to a stop at the next station, she and the old man got off together. As they strode to the platform, she looked over at him, but he was staring straight ahead.

The man told her to wait while he walked over and said something to the man in the subway ticket booth. Then he returned to where she was standing.

"My dear," he said after a pause. "I'm sorry to alarm you, but it was absolutely necessary that you got off that train immediately."

"B-but why?" Sarah asked. "I mean that

guy in the blue suit seemed weird and all. But he didn't seem like he'd hurt me. He just stared. Maybe it was a nervous habit. And his friend seemed too whacked out to do anything."

"It was no nervous habit," the man answered. "And the man with him was certainly not his friend. You see, I'm a doctor. I know what it means when I see someone with that look in his eye."

"What do you mean? Was he sick? Or blind?"

The man shook his head. "I'm sorry to have to tell you this," he said. "The man in the blue suit was a corpse."

Sarah gasped.

"And there's more," the man said. "From where I was waiting on the platform, I could see that there was a knife in his back. I got on the train to warn you."

"Oh no!" Sarah had started to tremble uncontrollably.

The man smiled grimly. "I think we've just seen the subway slasher in action. And if I hadn't been able to warn you in time, you might have become his next victim!"

Horror Weekend

IT was time for the part of camp that junior counselors Brad Evans and Tom Benson liked the best. It was Horror Weekend, the weekend that Brad and Tom got to scare the daylights out of the new campers. On Friday night, the boys would tell their new campers a round of ghost stories—including the creepiest story of them all—the story of the old Tolliver place.

The story was a really good one. The old Tolliver mansion stood at the bend in the road near the entrance of the camp. The parents of a boy named Mac Tolliver once owned all the land that the camp stood on. When they fell into hard times, they had had to sell off the land to the camp. Poor Mac lost his mind. He had loved to explore the woods that were now camp property. He continued to play there for a while after his parents sold it, until one fateful summer day when he ran into two campers. The campers teased him and called him all kinds of horrible names. And then they beat him up.

The next day, the campers were found hanging from two trees near the house, their throats slashed. Mac's parents, the ones he blamed for selling his beloved woods to the camp, were found hanging in a bedroom of the old house, their throats slashed, too. Mac had written his name in blood on the bedroom wall, but no one ever heard from him again.

Brad and Tom had told the story so many times that they really didn't stop to think if it could be true. All they knew was that it was the perfect ghost story—especially because on Saturday night, the new campers would be spending the night in the old Tolliver mansion. All the counselors claimed, winking at each other, that the house was haunted by poor Mac Tolliver's ghost.

Of course, Brad and Tom had to spend some time trying to make the old mansion look haunted. But the job wasn't very tough. No one had lived in the Tolliver house for years, as far as they could tell. There were cobwebs over all of the doorways and hanging from the ceiling. All of the furniture was covered with grayish sheets. When the wind blew just right, it made a howling sound through the rafters. And every inch of the house creaked. You didn't have to try very hard to believe that Mac Tolliver—or the people he had killed—might come back someday.

But the boys livened the place up anyway. They fixed a branch against the window so that every time the wind blew, it would scratch at the pane. And they tape-recorded the sounds of screams and hid the tape-recorder underneath the cellar door. Then they took a knife and made scratch marks on the door inside the room where Mac's parents had been killed. When the house was all ready, they headed back to camp to tell the gruesome tale of Mac Tolliver!

The new campers were an assorted lot— three tough boys who didn't seem frightened of anything, a kid from Indiana who was twice as big as anyone else, and a genius type who had spent most of the first few days of camp playing with his calculator. And finally there was Cam Revillot. Cam was the perfect victim, Brad and Tom decided. He was easily startled—by something as simple as a walnut falling on the roof of the cabin. And he always seemed cold, too—Brad noticed that Cam was always shivering and rubbing his hands. His skin had a slightly greenish tint to it, too, as if he was almost always just about to get sick. Yep, Cam was the perfect victim. And Brad and Tom couldn't wait to scare the wits out of him.

That night, they told the story of the Tolliver murder around the campfire, and most of the boys just shrugged it off. Cam listened, his eyes wide. After the boys went off to the bunks, Brad and Tom noticed that Cam sat upright in his bed, his eyes blankly staring forward, until the counselors dozed off.

The next day, all the young campers woke up ready for the hike to the Tolliver place. No one seemed the least bit frightened—just anxious to get it over with. Only Cam seemed slightly excited, although he jumped when Brad blew the whistle for roll call.

Right after breakfast, though, Brad and Tom noticed that the boys seemed a bit flushed. Everyone but Cam, that is, who was still complaining about how cold it was in the cabin. As they got their gear ready, the boys one by one turned green, and then disappeared into the bathroom. Before Brad and Tom knew it, everyone seemed to have a severe case of the stomach flu. Only Cam seemed to be unaffected by the flu. And compared to the way that the other boys looked, he seemed downright healthy!

Brad and Tom shook their heads in disappointment.

"I guess we'll have to cancel Horror Weekend," Brad said to Tom in a low voice.

"It'll be the first time in 10 years that a camper hasn't slept in the Tolliver mansion," Tom said. "And this is probably my last year as a counselor."

"I guess it's just as well," Brad said. "The only kid who would really be scared is Cam over there—and he's the only one healthy enough to go."

"Are you thinking what I'm thinking?" Tom asked with a sly smile on his face.

"Tom, you've got to be kidding! It's bad enough to have a whole bunch of campers spend the night at the Tolliver place—but to send poor Cam over by himself—that just wouldn't be fair. He'd die of fright for sure!"

"Well," Tom said, with a wicked grin on his face. "Cam wouldn't have to be alone. I could go with him, you know. Then I could make it really scary. You could stay here with the sickies."

"If you ask me, you're the sickie," Brad answered.

"Come on, Brad," Tom pleaded. "This is my last chance to really scare someone. And this

Cam—well, he'd be great to scare. He's such a little snot nose, after all."

"Well, he is kind of a wimp. And all he does is complain," Brad agreed. "But maybe you shouldn't go out there by yourself. You know, they never found Mac Tolliver."

"Oh, come on, Brad. It's just a story, remember?" Tom asked, shaking his head. "Geez, you're worse than that little wimp, Cam." Tom looked at Brad. "And besides," he said, "I'd rather be there than here with a bunch of barfing brats."

"Okay, you win," Brad said. "Take Cam and get going. We'll see you at breakfast tomorrow morning. That is, if any of these guys can stomach breakfast by then."

Brad watched as Tom gathered up his things and headed for the door. Tom didn't have to work on Cam very hard to get him to go. By that time, the cabin was full of sick kids. Cam seemed pretty happy to get out of there. As they headed down the path, Tom winked at Brad.

The day wore on, and the campers seemed to be getting better. By 4:00, they were all talking about the Tolliver place. They begged and pleaded with Brad to take them there. If they hurried, they said they could make it before dark. Brad looked around at the group.

He had to admit that he was pretty disappointed himself about missing the highlight of Horror Weekend. And besides, he felt sorry for Tom, having to spend the night there by himself with that sniffling Cam. He'd probably end up wiping the kid's nose all night—and that was no way to spend your last summer at camp!

Brad gave in. The kids loaded up their gear and the whole gang headed out of the door. The hike would take a couple of hours and nightfall was coming soon. But there was a full moon, so the hike wasn't as tough as it could have been. Brad led the way, talking about the Tolliver story as they walked. He told them Mac Tolliver could still be around—in the woods, behind the next rock—anywhere! He reminded them that the ghosts of the dead campers could be heard on the night of the full moon—screaming for their lives, begging for mercy!

Just as he mentioned the screaming, the mansion came into view and a cry broke the night. *Perfect timing,* Brad thought to himself. The campers looked at each other, and then shook their heads.

"Aw, he rigged the whole thing," the kid from Indiana said.

"Yeah," another kid added. "He timed our entrance perfectly."

Just then they heard another scream—this one sharper than the first—coming from the second floor of the old house. Brad grinned. *Tom sure is hamming it up for Cam,* he thought.

Brad led the boys to the front door of the house. As he touched the knob, he heard a groan from the upstairs room and slow, creaking footsteps. *That Tom!* he thought to himself and glanced at the campers. "You guys game?" he asked.

"Yeah," said one of the tough kids. "This is just hocus-pocus junk. Let's go inside and prove it."

"He's right," said his buddy. "Who's afraid of this corny stuff? I've seen scarier stuff right outside my window in the city!"

The group entered the house slowly. Except for a few creaking floorboards, the house was silent. The screaming had stopped.

"See," said the kid from Indiana. "Nothing here. I knew it was all sound effects."

Just then, there came a *thump-thump-thump* sound from upstairs.

"Tom?" Brad called, heading for the stairs. "Cam?"

The *thump-thump-thump* came again.

"Hey," Brad said. "You guys cut that out. Are you up there or what?"

"Yeah, right," said one of the kids. "You expect us to believe that something weird's going on? You must think we're pretty stupid."

But the thumping sound continued.

"The best thing to do," said the nerd, "is to investigate."

"You guys stay here," Brad said. "I'll go first." Brad started up the stairs.

"Hey, wait for us," the kid from Indiana said, following him.

The thumping became louder.

"Yeah!" said the rest of the kids. The sound of their voices echoed through the old house.

Brad climbed the stairs, the rest of the boys at his heels. He figured that this was one of Tom's pranks, but he couldn't shake the feeling that something wasn't quite right. After all, Tom hadn't even known they were coming. How could he have set something like this up so quickly? And where was that Cam kid, anyway? He wasn't the kind of kid who would have helped Tom play this kind of prank.

They were at the top of the steps now, following the sound. It was getting louder, and it seemed to be coming from the bedroom at the end of the hall—the bedroom where Mac Tolliver had killed his parents.

Brad reached for the doorknob. *Thump, thump*—the sound kept on coming. But now there was another strange sound with it— one that sounded like water dripping. Brad turned the knob and held his breath. The boys snickered, but it was a nervous kind of laughter.

Brad opened the door. Then he and the campers screamed. Hanging in front of them from a noose was Tom. His body was swinging, ever so slightly, making thumping sounds against the wall opposite the door. Blood was dripping from Tom's throat.

"He's faking," one of the kids said. "That's fake blood."

But when Brad slowly approached the body and looked into Tom's open, bulging, staring eyes, he could tell that he was dead. Brad shook his head in disbelief and horror. And when he looked at the rest of his body, he could tell how Tom had died.

His neck had been slashed just like the Tollivers' had been 10 years earlier.

The campers had realized what had happened. A few were crying softly.

"But who? How?" Brad stammered.

His question was soon answered. On the wall, written in blood—Tom's blood—was the name CAM REVILLOT. The bloody letters reflected in the mirror of the dresser across the room told Brad all he needed to know.

Mac Tolliver had come back. And he had claimed his revenge once more.

Midnight

MARCIE Simpson didn't really like to baby-sit for her sister Julie and her husband, Dave. It wasn't their six-month-old baby, Thomas, that she didn't like. She thought Thomas was the sweetest baby she'd ever seen. It was their house. It was way out in the country, up on a hill, deep in the woods. There were a couple of houses nearby, but Marcie felt isolated—out in the middle of nowhere—whenever she visited there.

It wasn't a bad house really. Right after Dave and Julie had moved in, though, it had burned almost to the ground. It had been a terrible fire, and Dave and Julie had lost just about everything. Marcie had been away at camp at the time, but her mom had called her. "They were lucky to escape with their lives," her mom had said. Marcie's eyes had filled with tears at the thought.

They had rebuilt the house after that fire, and Marcie knew how hard it had been on her sister. It was as if her sister was always waiting for something else to happen, as if she could never relax, as if something horrible waited just around the corner.

Marcie tried to put those thoughts out of her mind that night as she watched her sister and brother-in-law pull out of the driveway. A storm was rumbling in the distance. That was all she needed. First, to be way out here where no one could hear her if she screamed, and now a storm. *Oh, well, at least the phone works,* Marcie thought. *Things could be worse.*

Thomas was already asleep when she arrived so Marcie went upstairs to check on him. She tucked his blue baby blanket around his shoulders and then she headed downstairs, lay down on the couch, and began reading her battered copy of *Let's Be Friends Forever.* She tried to ignore the thunder outside and the lightning, too. But they seemed to be getting closer and closer. Maybe she should call her mom. That would make her feel better. Her mom always made her feel better during a storm.

She picked up the phone.

The line was dead.

It was then that she heard it. Between the

crashes of thunder, there was a low moan. Marcie shook her head, sure she was imagining things. The thunder crashed again outside. The lights flickered, and then went out.

And then she heard the sound again. It was almost like a growl, but not exactly. It sounded like an animal of some sort—an animal in hideous pain. In the darkness, she strained her ears to try to tell where the sound was coming from. It seemed to be coming from somewhere above her, upstairs maybe. She shuddered.

The sound was coming from little Thomas's room.

Her heart pounding, she stumbled across the room to the phone. She picked it up. It was still dead. Another crash of thunder sounded. Then there was another low moan, almost a wail this time.

Marcie knew that she had to figure out where the sound was coming from—she had to see if Thomas was in danger. She pulled the pantry door open and grabbed a candlestick. She remembered that her sister had stored them there last Christmas. And there was still a nub of a candle left. She left the pantry and headed to the fireplace. She remembered that there were fireplace matches on top of the mantel. She fumbled along the top of the mantel until she felt them. And then she heard the moan again, only it was louder this time. And it was coming from the top of the steps. Whatever it was stood between her and Thomas. She had to go up there. She had to make sure Thomas was safe.

Slowly, she climbed the stairs, the candle in her hand. She hesitated as she reached the landing. Then she heard the growl again. She held the candle high as she turned the corner. She gasped as she saw what was in front of her.

It had yellow eyes, eyes that glowed in the dark. And it was covered with fur. She held the light closer as the creature growled again.

It was a dog—a black Labrador retriever, its eyes shining in the darkness. The dog growled again, and turned its head, pointing toward the open door of Thomas's room. It seemed to be growling at Thomas. Or was it growling at her? She took a step toward Thomas's bed. The dog put its head down and made a low groan, its eyes glowing even more strangely.

Finally, Marcie found the courage to use her voice. "W-w-where'd you come from, boy?" she asked, her voice shaking. "It's okay. I'm Thomas's aunt. I'm not going to hurt him."

Strangely enough, the dog seemed to understand. It raised its head up and nudged her knees. Then it licked her palm. Marcie let out a sigh of relief.

Marcie knew that Julie had wanted a dog for a long time, but Dave didn't seem to want one. "I guess she finally got her way," Marcie said to herself. But where had the dog come from? Where had it been hiding? Why hadn't she seen it in Thomas's room before?

It must have been sleeping in the closet, Marcie figured, as she called to the dog and quietly shut Thomas's door.

"Hey, boy, what's your name?" she asked the black dog as he nuzzled her face.

There was a leather braided collar around its neck with a tag dangling from it that said *Midnight.*

"Well, come on, Midnight," Marcie said. "You can keep me company." And the two of them headed downstairs. Marcie settled down with her book again and tried to concentrate. But she hadn't finished the first paragraph when she heard Midnight growling again.

He was standing straight at attention and sniffing the air.

"Something wrong, Midnight?" she asked.

Midnight looked at her and whined. Then he began growling again. The storm outside was really raging and she was stuck way out in the country with a baby and a dog that was acting crazy. Didn't they say dogs acted this way when they had rabies or something?

Midnight turned his head in the direction of the stairs.

"Should I check on Thomas again, boy? Is that it?"

Midnight barked as if to say yes and turned to go upstairs.

This is really weird, Marcie thought to herself.

She followed Midnight upstairs.

When she got to Thomas's room, he was sound asleep, his little hands curled around a teddy bear. His blanket hung through the bars of the baby crib. Marcie stroked his head and turned to Midnight. "See, Midnight," she said. "He's okay. Nothing to worry—"

But Midnight had grabbed the edge of Thomas's blanket with his teeth and was pulling on it. Thomas woke up, rolling his sleepy eyes toward Marcie and reaching his arms up.

"See what you did, Midnight, you woke him up!" Marcie said angrily. But Midnight was whining again and turning his head toward the steps. Something in the dog's eyes made her think he was trying to tell her something. But what? This was crazy!

"What are you trying to say, Midnight? Do

60

you think Thomas wants to—"

Just then, she saw a flash of lightning that lit up the entire house.

"Okay, Midnight. We'll go downstairs if that's what you want."

Midnight ran ahead, with Thomas's blanket in his mouth as Marcie carried Thomas down the stairs.

As soon as they reached the living room, Midnight began barking at the door.

"What is it now, Midnight, do you want to go out?" Midnight just barked louder, with a real urgency. Then he began to howl and jump around, his claws making strange tapping sounds on the hardwood floor.

Marcie, still holding Thomas, opened the door for Midnight. And, just as she did, she saw a brilliant flash, followed by a crack of thunder. And then she smelled a peculiar smell, like toast burning, only, only . . .

Suddenly she knew what had happened. Lightning had struck the house! They had to get out before the house burned down around them.

Marcie didn't stop for raincoats or umbrellas. She bounded outside, behind Midnight. With Thomas clutched to her chest, she ran down the driveway for what seemed to be an eternity. Behind her she smelled smoke, and when she dared to turn and look around, she saw that the entire house was in flames. When she got to the main road, she flagged a car down. She hadn't noticed in the dark that it was Dave's car.

"Dave, Julie," she said, out of breath. "We just got out in time. The house was hit by lightning. It's, it's . . ."

But she didn't need to say any more. From the road, through the trees, Julie and Dave could see that the house was on fire. And before they could even think about heading down to the main road to call the fire department, they heard the wail of sirens and saw the flashing of lights through the woods. Dave hopped out of the car and ran up the driveway to help the firemen.

Julie took Thomas in her arms and gave Marcie a hug. "All that matters is that you two are all right. I don't know what I would have done if you hadn't made it."

"We barely got out in time," Marcie said breathlessly. She started to shake when she realized what had almost happened to her and Thomas.

Marcie continued, "If it hadn't been for Midnight . . . Hey, what happened to Midnight, anyway? He was right in front of us when we left the house. He's the one who told us to get out of there. I mean it, Julie, it was just incredible! He actually saved our lives."

But Julie's face had lost all of its color.

"Don't worry, Julie," Marcie said. "It's only a house, you know, I mean, the most important thing is that Thomas is safe. I'm sure the firemen . . ."

"This Midnight," Julie said. "Was it a dog, a black Labrador, about three years old?"

"Yeah. He was in your house. Where'd he go? He was right here a second ago. Julie," Marcie added, "Midnight is your dog, isn't he?"

Julie just shook her head. Tears were streaming down her cheeks as she pulled Thomas close to her. She couldn't speak for several moments.

"Midnight *was* our dog," Julie said when she was able to speak. "He was a stray that just showed up at our door. It was weird—a full-blooded dog like that is worth some money, you know? But he just came around and never left. It was sort of like he belonged there.

"The only reason we didn't get rid of him was because he really seemed to love Thomas. The minute we brought Thomas home from the hospital, Midnight began lying right underneath his bed. And when Thomas would cry, he'd pull his blanket out of his bed and bring it to us—as if to tell us that we should check on him. And any time someone came to the house that Midnight hadn't met, he was really protective, like he was looking out for Thomas."

Julie stopped for a second to catch her breath. She shook her head. "It just couldn't be, Marcie. It just couldn't be," she said, her voice barely above a whisper.

"Why couldn't it be the same dog?"

"Because . . . ," Julie said, "because Midnight died in the first fire we had. I never should have locked him in the kitchen, but Dave was worried he'd make a mess in the house. So I shut him in there and, when the fire started, he couldn't get out. We found him after the fire, charred. The only thing that we could recognize was his leather collar and name tag. It couldn't have been the same Midnight that you saw," she added after a pause. "It must have been a different dog, a different stray."

"But, Julie, I know it was the same dog. He seemed to know Thomas. He even took Thomas's blanket in his mouth when we left the house. Couldn't he have escaped the first fire or something?"

"Marcie, Midnight is dead. We buried his remains right by the barn over there." She pointed to the barn on the other side of the house. "At least the barn will be spared."

"Where's his grave, Julie? I need to see it. I know he's alive! I just know it!"

"Marcie, tomorrow. Tomorrow I'll show you."

"No, Julie, now! I want to see it now! I can't believe that the dog that saved our lives is dead."

"Okay, go ahead. It's over there, right by the well. There's a small gravestone. Just stay out of the way of the firemen."

Trembling, Marcie headed up the hill. The fire roared in the distance and she could hear the shouts from the firemen, the spray of the water, the static of their radio.

As she approached the place Julie had pointed out, she felt a shiver go up her back. She heard a low growl.

"Midnight?"

She looked down at his little gravestone and gasped. The dirt on the grave was fresh, not grass-covered, and there were dog tracks on either side of it. But the thing she saw next scared her most of all.

There, on top of Midnight's grave, was Thomas's blue baby blanket.

The Sea of the Dead

KAITLIN Thompson loved living by the seashore. Every day Kaitlin walked to school right by the ocean. She would walk across the beach, her book bag over her shoulder, and take in the salty smell of a new morning. Then she'd come to a pier where the fishermen were preparing to go out for the day. Sometimes she'd stand at the end of the pier and watch them loading their boats with nets and bait. Most people would have hated that yucky, fishy smell, especially in the morning. But Kaitlin loved it.

There was another reason that Kaitlin liked to watch the fishermen in the morning. She particularly liked one of the fishermen. Kenny Roberts was 23, and blond, with twinkling blue eyes. Kaitlin knew that nothing would ever really come of her crush on Kenny. After all, she was only in seventh grade.

Kaitlin was thinking about Kenny one warm spring morning as she skipped down the beach toward school. Even though it was warm and sunny, there were dark clouds piling up in the distance, and the humid air suggested that a storm was brewing. As she came closer to the pier, she smoothed down her hair a little so that she'd look good in case Kenny was around.

"Hey, Kaitie," she heard from the other end of the pier. It was Kenny's voice. She felt her heart stop for just a minute, and then yelled back.

"Hey, yourself," she called, walking to the end of the pier and looking down into Kenny's boat.

He looked up at her with those piercing blue eyes and, for a second, Kaitie felt as if she would faint.

"How do you think the fishing will be today? Looks like the wind is picking up," Kaitie managed to say.

"Yep, there's a big storm coming out of the east," Kenny answered. "Might have to come in early. Last storm almost took old *Betsy Blue* here," he said, pointing to his boat. "How about you, Kaitie? What do you have going today?"

"Got a big science test today," Kaitie

68

answered with a smile. "Maybe I should just skip school and come out fishing with you today."

"I don't think your parents would like that, Kaitie. But hey, how about if I give you my special charm, just for luck. Then maybe you'll do okay on your test."

Kenny held out his closed hand. Kaitie laughed. It was a joke between the two of them. Kenny had one special good luck charm that he kept with the boat at all times—it was a gold coin that he had recovered scuba diving from a wrecked galleon in the Florida Keys. But he had lots of other coins—pennies, dimes, nickels, and quarters. And he would always try to pawn these off as his special good luck charm. But Kaitie knew the real charm never left the boat. It seemed like all the fishermen were superstitious, so she respected Kenny's feelings. And she always took the coin he offered anyway, as if it held some sort of special power.

Kaitie did okay on her science test, but she couldn't shake the feeling that something was wrong with Kenny. The feelings became especially strong toward the end of the class period when the wind came up and lightning began to flash outside. *This must be the storm Kenny was worried about,* Kaitlin thought to herself. *I hope he's brought* Betsy *in by now.*

When the bell rang, Kaitie ran for the door. She grabbed her coat from her locker and headed straight to the beach. Again, she felt those awful feelings. Something was wrong with Kenny, each of her steps seemed to be saying. "Please let him be all right," Kaitlin asked out loud. "Please let him be all right."

When she got to the pier, she saw a few other boats docking and fishermen hurrying around battening their boats down for the storm. But there was no sign of Kenny or the *Betsy Blue.*

Kaitlin couldn't help worrying about Kenny. She went home and tried to eat dinner with her family, but her stomach felt too weird. She tried to study, but she couldn't concentrate. And at 9:00, the storm blew out all the electricity, so she couldn't watch TV either. She had no choice but to go to bed. But she spent the night tossing and turning and worrying about Kenny.

The next morning she got up extra early. She knew that Kenny was always the first one down at the docks. She got dressed quickly and hurried down to the pier. *He just has to be there,* she told herself. *He just has to . . .*

She headed down the beach, first walking quickly and then practically running all the way. And when she got closer to the pier, she felt her heart skip a beat. There, on the end of the dock, was Kenny and he was motioning for her to come closer.

"Kenny!" she yelled as she approached him. "I was so worried, I thought you'd been lost in the storm!"

When she looked in his eyes, there was no twinkle, only a dull stare, as if he had fallen asleep with his eyes open.

"Kenny?" Kaitlin asked. "Are you okay? Where's *Betsy Blue*?"

But Kenny just stared ahead, as if he had barely heard her.

"Did you lose her, Kenny? Did you lose your boat in the storm?"

He nodded slowly.

"Well, that's okay," Kaitlin said nervously. "I'm just glad you're safe. You can get a new boat and it will probably be better than *Betsy Blue*. It will be newer and you can fix it up real nice and . . ."

She stopped. He was holding out a closed hand to her.

"Oh, Kenny!" Kaitlin said. "I don't need another good luck charm. I think I did well on the test. And I won't have to worry about science again until exam time."

Kenny just nodded slowly and held out his

hand again. She reached for his hand and took the coin he held. And she watched as Kenny turned and walked toward the beach.

"Kenny," Kaitlin yelled. "I've got to go to school. But thanks! And tomorrow we'll talk more about . . ."

But he was already out of sight.

Kaitlin headed to school with a sigh. *At least he's okay,* she thought to herself. *But why was he acting so weird?*

When she got to school, she started to put the good luck charm in her locker. But then she noticed it wasn't the usual dime or nickel. This was the special gold coin itself—the one that Kenny always kept on the boat. *Why would he give me this one?* she asked herself. Maybe it means something. Maybe it means he really likes me, even though I'm only in seventh grade. She turned the gold coin over and over in her hands and then she held it up to the light. She noticed that it was covered with some greenish material—almost like moss.

She put the coin in her pocket. It was too precious to keep in her locker. She carried it around with her the whole day. Every once in a while, she'd reach into her pocket and run her fingers along the coin's rough edges. She rubbed the green moss, too. But the moss didn't come off on her hands. She couldn't even wash it off of the coin in the sink in the girls' restroom at lunch time.

"This is really weird," Kaitlin said. "Too weird. I better ask Mr. Gray what's going on." She walked quickly to the science lab. Mr. Gray looked up when she came through the door.

"If this is about your science test, Kaitlin, I haven't gotten around to grading it yet."

"No, Mr. Gray, it's about this weird stuff that's growing on this coin. I figured if anyone knew what it was, it would be you."

She handed the coin to Mr. Gray. He scratched his head. "Hmmm," he said. "Where did this come from?"

"Kenny Roberts gave it to me this morning. I didn't notice the green stuff growing on it until I got to school."

Mr. Gray's face turned white. "Kenny Roberts gave you this, you say? This morning?"

Kaitie nodded. "Down by the pier. He acted kind of weird. I guess he was upset about losing his boat in the storm last night. I'm just glad he's all right . . ."

Mr. Gray looked Kaitie straight in the eyes. "Kaitie, I want you to tell me the truth about this. I know that you're probably pretty upset about Kenny, but . . ."

Kaitie shook her head in confusion. "Mr. Gray, I am telling you the truth. I saw Kenny this morning and he gave me this coin. And then I noticed this green stuff on it. Why would I lie about that?"

"Kaitie, this isn't just any green stuff. It's a special sea fungus. It reproduces very rapidly, especially when it has something to feed on."

"What do you mean, something to feed on?" Kaitie asked.

"Kaitie, sit down, I need to tell you something."

Kaitie sat down, still confused.

"Kenny Roberts died in the storm last night. It was on the news this morning. His boat was demolished when it ran against the cliff over at Sunnyside. Kenny is dead."

"But . . . ," Kaitie said in disbelief. "I saw him this morning, I know I did. He gave me this coin. It's his good luck piece."

"Kaitie," Mr. Gray said. "His body washed up on the beach. Kenny's definitely dead. I'm sorry to have to tell you this. Maybe I should call your parents and they can come and take you home."

By now, Kaitie was in tears.

"Kaitie," Mr. Gray said. "I'm going to call your parents now to come and get you—"

"But Mr. Gray, just tell me one more thing.

The stuff on the coin, where did it come from?"

Mr. Gray looked at Kaitie tenderly and said, "Kaitie, I don't know where it came from or how it got there, but it's a rare kind of sea fungus. A fungus," Mr. Gray paused, "that only grows on dead people."

Killer Cactus

THE minute Dawn saw the cactus, she knew it was perfect for their apartment. She and her husband, Joel, had just moved from her parents' house into their own place. They didn't have much furniture, mostly stuff from Goodwill or hand-me-downs from relatives. She wanted to buy something—anything—that would make their apartment feel like their very own. And that great cactus just might do it.

It didn't really look like a cactus. It had broad green leaves, with tiny little spines. And it was almost five feet tall! The sign next to it in the plant store claimed that it didn't need much light or water. It would be perfect in their new apartment—in the corner of the living room! Dawn didn't have a whole lot of money, but she pulled what she had from her wallet and proudly carried the cactus home.

As she brought the cactus into their apartment, she heard a strange sound—sort of a humming, from inside the thick cactus stem. She shook her head and the sound went away. She figured that she had imagined it—or maybe that she was just feeling a little light-headed from carrying the huge plant half a block.

When Joel got home, he was thrilled. He agreed that it was just the thing to make their apartment really special. He helped Dawn put it in the corner of the living room. The apartment really had a homey feeling, as if it were a special place the two of them could share for all time.

Their cats were curious about the cactus. Seymour, the smaller of the two cats, rubbed up against the pot that held the cactus, but bristled when he felt the small, sharp needles. Clarissa, the fat Siamese, liked to lie in the shade of the plant's branches, sometimes reaching up to lazily bat at one of its broad leaves.

One morning when Dawn woke up, she noticed that Clarissa didn't look well. Clarissa usually met Dawn at breakfast and insisted on lapping up the milk from her cereal bowl when she was finished. But that morning, Clarissa just lay in the corner under the plant and refused to move.

By noon, Dawn was really worried about the cat and called Joel at work. Joel's reaction was his usual one—so the cat's too lazy to eat, what's the big deal? But when he came home, he realized why Dawn was so worried. Clarissa could barely move. And Seymour was acting sluggish, too.

Joel and Dawn put both cats into the car and headed to the vet.

When the vet saw Clarissa, he was very concerned. Her vital signs were very, very weak. Seymour was acting fairly frisky, so the vet suggested that they leave Clarissa there and take Seymour home. He'd call them in the morning and give a full report.

But Clarissa didn't live till morning. Sometime during the night, she passed away with the vet standing by helplessly. He just couldn't figure out what was wrong with the cat.

The vet called the next day and Dawn was very upset by the news. But she was more upset because Seymour was now showing the same symptoms that Clarissa had earlier. He was lying lazily underneath the plant, barely able to move. The cats were practically all she and Joel had, she said to the vet between sobs—the cats and the plant. The rest of their things were all hand-me-downs.

Dawn could tell by the sound of the vet's voice that he understood. Some people, the vet said, love animals more than they think they do. And, when they lose them, it's as hard as losing a human being that they love.

But the vet had something more important on his mind. "Get Seymour in here quick!" he said. "Meanwhile, I'll do an autopsy on Clarissa. If we can find out what killed her, perhaps we can save Seymour."

Sobbing, Dawn and Joel carried Seymour to the car. As they drove to the vet, Seymour curled up in Dawn's lap and just went limp.

The vet had just started the autopsy on Clarissa when Dawn and Joel got there. There was nothing they could do to help, he explained. It was best for them to leave Seymour with him and go home and try to relax. He told them to wait for his call.

Reluctantly, Dawn and Joel agreed that the vet was right. They climbed into the car and headed home.

They tried to relax in front of the TV, but they had trouble settling down. Every time Dawn saw a commercial for cat food, she burst into tears. Joel tried not to show it, but he was upset, too. Seymour had been his cat since he was in high school. He couldn't bear to lose him now.

Joel looked over at the corner where the cactus was, imagining Seymour taking his nap beneath it. As he thought about it, the plant began to move.

Joel closed his eyes and opened them again, to be sure of what he had seen. The plant was still moving, ever so slightly, shaking just a little bit.

He looked back at the TV.

He looked back at the plant. It was still shaking.

He looked at Dawn. He could tell she had noticed it, too, but was pretending that she hadn't. Her eyes were glued to the TV screen, but every once in a while, they'd dart to the corner where the plant stood, linger there a second, and then move back to the TV set.

"Dawn," Joel said after a few minutes. "What's with the plant?"

"What plant?"

"You know, that weird cactus you bought. Is it moving or isn't it?"

Dawn and Joel both looked at the plant. The plant was shaking back and forth now. It was definitely moving.

"It's shaking a little," Dawn said. "Maybe that's because it's near the heater vent or something . . ."

Just then the plant shook a little more violently and a strange humming noise filled the apartment.

"Dawn," Joel said. "You better call the plant store. That plant is acting weird—that is if a plant can act weird."

"But Joel," Dawn said. "I don't want to tie up the phone line. The vet might try to call."

Joel shook his head. "I'm not staying in this apartment with that plant one more night. The next thing you know it's going to be dancing on the rug or something. If you won't call, I will."

Joel watched as Dawn picked up the phone and dialed the number of the plant store. She inquired about the plant, and then her face went white. She dropped the phone.

"Joel," she said, "we've got to get out of here! Now!"

"Come on, Dawn. I was only kidding. It's only a plant."

"Joel, I mean it, NOW!"

When they were out on the street, Dawn told Joel what the man at the plant store had told her.

"Those cacti . . . ," she said, gulping her breaths. "They're imported from Mexico and they're . . ."

"They're what?"

82

"They're full of eggs . . ."

"Eggs? Come on, Dawn. What kind of eggs?"

"Tarantula eggs! That's what the guy at the plant store said. And he said that they were just about ready to hatch. That we had to get out of there."

"Dawn, you're imagining things. How could he sell something like that?"

"He didn't know about the eggs until a couple of customers called to complain. Then he investigated and had all of the plants in stock destroyed. But he couldn't track down everyone who had bought one of the plants."

"I don't know, Dawn."

"I know it sounds weird, but—"

Joel interrupted. "Do you think that this might have anything to do with . . ."

"Clarissa's death?" Dawn thought for a second. "How could it have?"

"There's only one way to find out. Let's head to the vet's office right now!"

Dawn and Joel ran to the car and sped all the way to the vet's office. They rang the night bell and, after a few minutes that seemed like hours, the vet came to the door.

"Oh," he said, looking relieved. "I was just trying to call you. I think that Seymour is out of danger. It's a good thing that I performed that autopsy on Clarissa. We might never have found out what was wrong."

"Doctor," Joel said, "what exactly was wrong?"

"It was like nothing I've ever seen before. Somehow, Clarissa and Seymour ate some tarantula eggs. In Clarissa's case, they hatched. I hardly know how to tell you this." The vet took off his glasses and rubbed his eyes.

"The baby spiders started eating their way out of her stomach."

Dawn and Joel gasped.

"And, in Seymour's case, we operated just in time to remove the eggs before they hatched. If we had waited any longer, he never would have made it. He would have died the same way."

Dawn's and Joel's faces turned sheet-white.

"Do you have any idea how the cats got a hold of these eggs?" the vet asked. "It's a rather rare form of tarantula that lays its eggs by boring a tiny hole in a cactus plant."

Joel and Dawn could only stare at each other in disbelief. They knew all too well where the tarantula eggs had come from. And they knew they couldn't go home . . .

The Man with the Skeleton Face

JEFF hated to go camping. And he especially hated to go camping in the rain. When his buddies Doug and Jon had suggested the idea last week, he'd tried to talk them out of it. But they were determined to go. They had promised to meet him at the campground on Kelley's Island at 7:00 on Friday night. Now it was 8:30 and they still weren't there.

Where are those guys? Jeff asked himself. Jeff had taken the early afternoon ferry over. The last ferry ran at 6:00—if Doug and Jon hadn't caught that ferry, they wouldn't make it. And Jeff would be stuck at the campground all by himself. Even the ranger who had been there earlier had left. And the rain had chased any other eager campers away. It was just Jeff, his tent, and some wet saltines. *Great,* he thought to himself, *just great! Boy, do I love camping!*

85

The rain was really picking up now, and there was lightning and thunder in the distance. As he listened to the sound of the rain on his tent in the empty campground, Jeff began to feel strange—not scared exactly—but anxious, as if something were about to happen.

He put those thoughts out of his mind and climbed in his sleeping bag. It was obvious that Doug and Jon weren't going to show up at this hour. He figured he might as well try to get some sleep. Tomorrow, he'd take the ferry back over to the mainland and try to find them.

As the wind whistled through the trees, Jeff kept trying to reassure himself. "I can make it through one night," he said aloud. It was only one night, after all, and he was no chicken.

It took Jeff a long time to fall asleep, and when he did, he didn't sleep very well. Every little noise seemed to waken him—the thunder in the distance, the scraping of the trees on the tent, the sound of horse hooves on the dirt road of the campground.

Horse hooves?

Jeff sat upright and shook himself to make sure that he was awake. Whatever sound he had heard had stopped. *It must have been a dream,* he told himself. Then he lay back down. But he heard the sounds again, and this time, they sounded too real to be a dream. *What would a horse be doing here, especially in the middle of the night?* he wondered.

Jeff opened the flap of his tent and looked outside. The rain had stopped, replaced by a heavy mist. There, in the mist, lit by a single lantern, was a black, horse-drawn cart. It looked like one of those old-fashioned hearses Jeff had seen carrying coffins in movies. Jeff's heart began to pound right through his chest. The hearse was heading his way.

As the hearse got closer, Jeff noticed a smell—a terrible smell. It was an odor he had smelled before, but where? Suddenly, it all came back to him—it was the smell of rotting flesh, the same odor he had smelled in his mother's kitchen. It had taken them weeks to figure out that the smell was coming from under the refrigerator. And when they moved the refrigerator, they discovered a dead rat underneath.

Jeff held his nose as the hearse drew closer. He noticed that there was a nameplate on the side of the cart—a nameplate reading C. Haron. But what Jeff saw next almost made him scream—there was a man dressed in a black suit driving the cart. Jeff couldn't see his face at first. Then the man leaned forward and Jeff gasped. His face was the most hideous sight he had ever seen. It was almost pure white, and his eyes were sunken in and hollow with red rims. It was almost as if the man were a living skeleton.

Jeff was too terrified to move. The man leaned forward in the carriage, with one arm outstretched, as if inviting Jeff inside. All Jeff could manage to do was to shake his head from side to side. Then he heard the man speak.

"Come," the man said in a slow, haunting voice. "It's time."

But Jeff shook his head again, his knees rattling together in his sleeping bag.

The man in the carriage just smiled, a horrible smile, with yellowed teeth and blood-red gums. He turned back to his team of black horses and took off into the night.

Jeff couldn't get out of his tent and sleeping bag fast enough. He ran to where the carriage had stood and looked at the ground. If the carriage had been real, there would be tracks from its wheels and there would be hoofprints from the horse hooves.

But there was nothing there—not a single track or hoofprint, nothing to show that it had been anything more than a dream.

Jeff didn't know whether to be relieved

because he thought he dreamed the whole thing or frightened because the incident had seemed too real to be a dream. He climbed back into his tent and sat up most of the night, trying to understand what had happened. When the sun came up the next day, he felt a little better. For one thing, he knew what he was going to do next—he was going straight home. He didn't care if Jon or Doug ever showed up at this point. He just had to get off of this island.

Jeff packed up his gear and trudged back to the ferry dock, trying to put what happened last night out of his head. But he couldn't stop thinking about it. It had seemed so real. And the terrible face on that man was unforgettable. As long as Jeff lived, he would remember that hideous face.

When Jeff got to the ferry, he bought a ticket at the ticket stand and waited under a little tarp for the ferry to come in. It looked like it would be a rough ride over. The lake was covered with whitecaps.

When the ferry arrived, Jeff boarded and settled down on a bench with his backpack and gear. He figured he'd take a nap on the way back to the mainland. After all, he didn't get much sleep the night before. It looked like he was going to be the only passenger on this ride. But that didn't surprise him. The island wasn't drawing much business in this awful weather.

All of a sudden, he heard a voice.

"Tickets, please."

Where had he heard that voice before? He opened his eyes and his heart went through his shoes.

It was him—the man with the skeleton face. He was wearing a black shirt this time, with his name, C. Haron, embroidered on it. The man with the skeleton face was the captain of the ferry! And he wanted Jeff's ticket. Jeff looked right, then left, then to the ferry dock. He didn't know how he was going to do it, but he had to get off the ferry.

"It's time," the man repeated. "Tickets, please."

Jeff rose to his feet and tried to get around the man. But the man with the skeleton face just laughed, his yellow teeth and blood-red gums bobbing up and down in a revolting motion.

The engines of the ferry began to rev.

Jeff took a step to the right. The man with the skeleton face took a step to the right and stood in Jeff's path.

Then the man said again, "It's time."

"No!" Jeff yelled.

Jeff grabbed the man by the collar and threw him down. The man writhed back and forth on the floor of the boat, just long enough for Jeff to jump over him.

The engines of the ferry were whirring—but there was no one at the helm. The ferry was pulling away from the dock by itself!

Jeff made it to the edge of the boat. There was more than a yard between him and the dock. Jeff dared to look back. The man with the skeleton face was coming toward him. His bony hand was almost on Jeff's shoulder. Jeff closed his eyes, held his breath, and jumped.

He barely made it. He felt the wooden slats underneath his feet. He had made it off the ferry. He had made it in time.

Jeff sat there on the edge of the dock for the rest of the morning. Every once in a while, his body began to shake when he tried to imagine what would have happened to him if he had stayed on that boat. He wasn't sure what he was going to do now. There was no way for him to get back to the mainland, unless he could hitch a ride with one of the fishermen. But most of them had already left for the day. When he felt that he could finally control the shaking, he wandered over to the fishermen's docks.

"Hey, Jeff!" he heard suddenly from one of

the boats that was just turning into the harbor. "HEY, JEFF!"

It was Doug's voice and it sounded strange—both urgent and relieved. As the boat got closer, Jeff could see that both Doug and Jon were aboard. And they were both waving frantically, as if they hadn't seen him in years.

"Hey, you guys! Where have you been?" Jeff asked as they got off the boat.

"We got held up last night. Doug spent too long saying good-bye to his girlfriend and we missed the last ferry," Jon answered.

"Never mind that," Doug said, giving his buddy a bear hug. "We're just glad you're safe. The news this morning said . . ."

"What's the morning news got to do with it?" Jeff asked. "Where were you last night? You know, it wasn't any fun spending the night alone at that campground."

"Well, when we missed the ferry last night," Jon picked up, "we figured that you'd head back to the mainland this morning to try and find us, only . . . only . . ."

"What? What happened?"

"Well, there was a problem with the ferry," Doug added. "And we were sure you were aboard . . ."

"Wait a minute, wait a minute," Jeff said.

"What problem with what ferry?"

"The morning ferry. Didn't you hear?"

"No," Jeff said slowly, "but I almost took it."

"You're lucky you weren't on it. It exploded just after it left the dock."

Jeff gasped. His legs failed him and he fell to the ground. Where would he be now if he hadn't gotten off the ferry when he did? And could the captain have been—no, Jeff couldn't even think about it—the captain couldn't have been the man with the skeleton face. It was a different captain, a different ferry. Jeff had dreamed the whole thing—the hearse, the skeleton face, all of it. It was too horrible to even think about.

But as Jeff listened to Jon and Doug talk, he knew he was wrong.

"The engine exploded and I guess the captain had his whole face blown off. I guess when they got to him he was practically a skeleton."

"A skeleton?" asked Jeff, trembling.

"Hey, what was the guy's name, Jon? I forget," said Doug.

Jon looked at Doug and shrugged. Then he answered, "Charles something. I think his name was Charles, Charles Haron."

About the Author

TRACEY E. DILS has always liked to tell stories—especially scary stories. When she was a little girl, she loved to terrify her family and friends with her own special brand of horror!

Tracey lives in a big, old Victorian house in Columbus, Ohio, with a dog, a cat, several fish, her husband, Richard, and her daughter, Emily. Some people think that Tracey's house is haunted. She's never seen any ghosts there, but she's sure that there's something scary in the basement. That's why she never goes down there alone!

Tracey is also the author of *Real-Life Scary Places*, published by Willowisp Press.